Poppy's Secret Wish

I was about to open the changing-room door when Jasmine whispered, "Good luck, Poppy."

She gave me a thumbs-up sign and I gave her one back. Then we held out our hands, pressed our thumbs together, and closed our eyes. We always do this. It's our secret wishing signal.

"Please, please, please *let us both be chosen," said Jasmine.*

I said it too, with every single bit of my whole body, inside and out.

Ballerina Dreams

Collect all the books in the series:

Jasmine's Lucky Star

Rose's Big Decision

Dancing Princess

Dancing with the Stars

Dancing For Ever

The Christmas Nutcracker

Ballerina Dreams

Poppy's Secret Wish

Ann Bryant

My sincerest thanks to Victoria Zafiropoulous
– Miss Victoria, the Principal of Tenterden Ballet Studio
– for her invaluable help, and for providing me with
inspiration for the character of Miss Coralie.
My thanks, also, to Rufina Hunn for her very astute help,
and to Sara Matthews, the Assistant Director of the Central
School of Ballet, for kindly allowing us to watch some classes.
And most of all, my thanks to Megan Larkin for
believing in me.

First published in the UK in 2004 by Usborne Publishing Ltd,
Usborne House, 83-85 Saffron Hill, London EC1N 8RT, England.
www.usborne.com

Cover photograph by Ray Moller.
Illustrations by Tim Benton.

A CPI catalogue record for this title is available
from the British Library.

JFMAM JASOND/07 ISBN 9780746060247 Printed in India.

1 Desperate to be Picked

Hi! I'm Poppy. I'm ten years old and I've got red hair and freckles. I'm the only one with red hair in my whole ballet class. You can't see much of it, thank goodness, by the time I've scraped it back and put on my ballet hairband. I wish I could scrape my freckles back too. That's only a small wish though. I don't mind them all that much really. My big wish is *much* more important.

"Why such a worried face, Poppy?" Mum was looking at me in the driving mirror.

"Because I *am* worried. Miss Coralie's going

to tell us who's doing the exam today. What if she doesn't pick me?"

My heart was doing the little popping thing it does when I'm nervous. Just thinking about Miss Coralie makes me go jittery.

"I'm sure you'll be fine."

"She might not think I'm good enough though."

"Then you can do it next time. It doesn't matter, does it? What's the rush?"

Mum didn't understand. She knows I really like ballet. In fact, she knows I *love* it. But she doesn't realize that it's the most important thing in my whole life. She's got no idea that I have daydreams of being the best in my class and getting specially picked to go to a proper ballet school – even though I know it could never happen in a trillion years.

And she doesn't know that sometimes I practise in my bedroom when I'm supposed to be fast asleep. I lie on top of the quilt and stretch my legs till it hurts.

I'd like to be as supple as Tamsyn Waters. She can do the splits front ways and sideways, and she can also lie on her tummy and curl herself backwards so her feet touch her nose. She's a bit of a show-off though.

Everyone knows that Tamsyn is sure to be picked for the exam, and then she'll go up to the next class with Jasmine.

"But I want to get into grade five, Mum. I don't want to be left behind because I'm not good enough."

"It doesn't mean you're not good enough if you don't get picked, Poppy," said Mum carefully. "It just means that you're not quite ready and that you'll probably be able to do it next term instead...or the one after."

I sighed. "That's ages and ages away. We've only just started *this* term. And anyway, it would mean I'm not good enough, because Miss Coralie keeps telling us that it's not only to do with how well we've learned the steps, it's to do with our whole attitude to ballet, and how much we practise and what our overall standard is like."

Mum was looking very serious. No wonder. There was nothing she could say, because I'd told the total truth and if I wasn't picked it meant I wasn't good enough. The end.

And, actually, it would feel like the end of my whole life. Nobody understands that because it's secret. Well, nobody except Jasmine Ayed. She's my friend from ballet.

Thinking about Jasmine made a little burst of words come zipping up my body and out of my mouth. "I can't wait till afterwards!"

Mum gave me a big smile in the mirror. "I'd better go home and get on with the tea when I've dropped you off, hadn't I? If Jasmine gets half as hungry as you do after ballet classes, I'm going to have a job fitting all the food on the table!"

I felt a bit babyish when Mum said that. She doesn't usually talk to me as if I'm a baby. I think she was just trying to keep my mind off this big important day. But it didn't work.

"I won't be in the same class as Jasmine if I don't get chosen, you know," I said in a bit of a whiny voice.

"Miss Coralie might well decide to keep you both in grade four, as you're so much younger than all the others."

"She won't keep Jasmine down, I bet."

"Well even if she doesn't, you'll still see each other."

"Only a bit. It's not like we go to the same school as each other."

"Well..." Mum's eyes were darting about now. She was looking for a parking space. "I'll just pull in here, love. Now, don't go getting yourself all worked up or you won't do your best." She turned round and gave me one of her firm smiles, as I call them.

I got out of the car and ran, with my dark blue bag banging against my side, to the big heavy door of The Coralie Charlton School of Ballet.

"Good luck!"

I only just heard Mum's voice because of the noise of the traffic on the High Street. Then I pushed open the door.

The smell of the entrance to the ballet school is the strongest smell I've ever smelled in a building – even stronger than the canteen at school. I don't really know what it is, but it always makes me think about an old castle that might have Rapunzel or someone imprisoned in it. The walls are cold and grey and it's a bit dark and dirty.

Your footsteps make a splitching, echoey sound when you run upstairs. I know there's no such word as splitching, but it's the best way to describe the noise. It's a spiral staircase, only with corners instead of bends, and it goes on and on and on. It's lovely when you've passed the first two corners and you can start to hear the voices of the other pupils up in the changing room. You can also hear the piano. It sounds plinky-plonky at first, but then it turns into a proper tune when you get nearer the top. It reminds me of a flower opening.

"Poppy!"

I leaned over the railing and saw Jasmine coming through the entrance down below. "Hi!" I called. "I'm really nervous. Are you?"

She nodded and her eyes looked all black and massive. "I couldn't find my tights and I thought Mum might have forgotten to wash them."

"Oh, no! Where were they?"

She giggled. "In my drawer. Same as usual." Then her voice went a bit shaky because she was rushing up the steps so fast. "I must be going blind."

As Jasmine ran, her ponytail swung from side

to side and spread out at the bottom like an upside-down fan. I'd give anything to have lovely black hair like Jasmine's. In fact, I wish I could swap looks with Jasmine altogether. Her skin is dark with not a freckle in sight. Jasmine says she'd rather look like me, but I know she only says it to make me feel better.

The moment she reached me, she clutched my arm. "We can practise for the exam when we get to yours, can't we?"

The jitters appeared in my tummy when she said that, and they whizzed round and round as we climbed the last few stairs. "What if I'm not picked, Jasmine?"

"You *will* be. You're good."

"Not as good as you."

"Yes, you are."

"I'm not. It's obvious."

"Well, *I* think you are."

"Well, Miss Coralie doesn't."

"It doesn't matter what Miss Coralie thinks.

She is only an ex-Royal Ballet dancer. *I'm* the important one around here!" We both broke into giggles. But Jasmine stopped immediately. We were nearly at the changing room.

"Oh, no!"

"What?"

"That's the *révérence* music, isn't it?"

Jasmine pronounced *"révérence"* the French way. It's the name of the curtsey step that you do at the end of the lesson. Her eyes were all big again because she thought the class before ours was just finishing and we were going to be late. But I recognized the music.

"It's okay, it's their dance. We've got ages."

I knew I sounded like someone who doesn't ever worry about *anything*, but inside me the jitters were spreading like mad. I was about to open the changing-room door when Jasmine whispered, "Good luck, Poppy."

She gave me a thumbs-up sign and I gave her one back. Then we held out our hands, pressed our thumbs together, and closed our eyes. We always do this. It's our secret wishing signal.

"Please, please, *please* let us both be chosen," said Jasmine.

I said it too, with every single bit of my whole body, inside and out.

There were quite a few girls getting changed, and one or two were eating crisps and doing *pliés.*

Tamsyn Waters was right in the middle of the room in a crab position. "Hi, Poppy! Hi, Jasmine!"

"How did you know it was us?" asked Jasmine.

Tamsyn uncurled smoothly and looked at herself in the mirror. "I recognized your feet." Then she arched one of her own feet and I saw a proud sort of smile go across her face.

Jasmine gave me a quick look. We both hate it when Tamsyn shows off about how supple she is.

"Oh, *no*!" screeched a girl called Sophie

Cottle. "I can't get this bump out of my hair. I'll have to start all over again!" Sophie's got very thick hair and it's layered, so it's practically impossible to make it lie flat and stay in place under her hairband. "Has anyone got any spare hairgrips?"

I handed her a few grips from the inside pocket of my bag, and felt happy that my hair is quite long and fine. It only breaks into curly bits at the bottom, so it's easy to bunch up into a bun. Mia, a friend in my class at school, says that where she goes for ballet lessons they can wear their hair loose if they want. That's because hers is the kind of dance school where they do stage-dancing and tap-dancing and things, and mine's more of a strict ballet school. Even its name sounds strict – The Coralie Charlton School of Ballet. Students do ballet right up to the age of sixteen, and one or two girls have even got into the Royal Ballet School from here.

When I'd got changed, and done up my shoes really neatly, and made sure every bit of my hair was tucked right inside my hairband, I whispered, "Shall we wait in the corridor?"

Jasmine nodded and we sneaked out of the changing room. I really wanted to get warmed up before the class started today. Then I'd be able to show Miss Coralie my very best steps right from the beginning of class. That might make her notice me and think I'd be good enough for the exam.

I could have warmed up in the changing room, I know, but I didn't want anyone to see me. Otherwise they'd all be thinking, *Look at Poppy Vernon! She must be absolutely* desperate *to do the exam.* Then, if Miss Coralie didn't pick me, everyone would probably stare at me and I'd go bright red and feel like bursting into tears.

"Are my feet rolling?" I asked Jasmine, as I went into a *plié* in first position.

She looked at them carefully, then shook her head. "Are mine?"

"You never roll, Jazz. I *so* wish I was as good as you."

"I'm only good at some things. I'm not half as good as you at actual dancing. Miss Coralie always says you've got lovely expression."

"She's talking about my top half."

"No, I'm sure she means all of you."

I was just about to say *I bet she doesn't*, when I heard the *révérence* music coming from behind the closed door of Room One.

"They're finishing! Help! I'm scared, Jasmine!" I hissed.

And at the very same moment, the changing-room door opened and all the others came out into the corridor. Jasmine and I did a quick thumb-thumb, down by our sides, where no one could see. Then we started to line up beside the door, first Jasmine, then me, then Tamsyn behind me.

"Why did you two come out here so early?" Tamsyn whispered into the back of my neck.

I turned my head and mouthed, "Just did," doing a sort of shrug at the same time.

Everyone knows you have to be in a silent line ready to file in the moment the other class has filed out.

The girls from the class before us came out looking hot and a bit pink. They didn't talk as they went past us. Miss Coralie doesn't have a rule about that. It's just better to wait till you get into the changing room. Then you can talk to your friend about how bad you were or how you didn't understand something.

I noticed that Jasmine was standing in fifth position. She always looks like a real ballerina. I tried it out, but I felt stupid because it doesn't suit me and my body, standing like that. That's because I haven't got such a good natural turnout as Jasmine. In fact, I haven't got such a good *anything* as her. Especially brain. When we do a sequence of steps, Jasmine can remember it straight away but it takes me ages.

I suddenly realized I was standing between a really brainy girl and a really supple girl. And what am *I* good at? Nothing. Except expression, and I'm sure that doesn't count half as much. It had probably been a waste of time getting warmed up extra well, because Miss Coralie would never pick me for the exam. I was so fed up, I felt like turning my feet inwards, rounding my shoulders, sticking my tummy out and dropping my head onto my chest.

"Come in, next class!"

This was it. The moment had arrived.

I stretched up tall, pulled my shoulders back and made a wish. *Please please please let me be picked.*

2 The New Girl

We always come in running with really light steps and go straight to a place on the *barre*. As I followed Jasmine, I noticed out of the corner of my eye that Miss Coralie was wearing her black swirly skirt, pale blue vest top, black cross-over and white tights. She had her black shoes on, the ones with little heels that looked totally like ordinary, flat ballet shoes on the top. I'm not sure how old she is – a bit older than Mum, I think. But she doesn't look like a mother. She looks...just perfect.

She was talking to Mrs. Marsden, the pianist,

but half-watching us at the same time. When we were all at the *barre*, she broke into a big smile and stood in first position with a really straight back. Then she let the smile go around the whole room, so every one of us got our own private bit of it.

"Good afternoon, girls," she said, putting her hand on an imaginary *barre* and lifting her chin a tiny bit. "*Pliés.* Fifth position…"

Mrs. Marsden was watching Miss Coralie carefully, waiting for the words: *Preparation... and…* Every single ballet exercise begins with these words. It's like an instruction for Mrs. Marsden to play the first note of the music and for us to be ready to start the exercise immediately.

We were all standing up as straight and tall as telegraph poles, staring at the back of the head of the girl in front, waiting for the magic words. But, instead of saying "*Preparation... and…*" Miss Coralie suddenly frowned and looked quickly around. "I thought the new girl was joining today. Is she not here?"

"New girl?" everyone whispered. "What new girl?"

I saw an impatient look flit across Miss Coralie's face. "A girl called Rose Bedford is joining the class. Has anyone seen her?"

Everyone shook their heads and I heard Tamsyn whisper, "Never heard of her."

I'd heard of her though. She goes to my school. In fact, she's in the same year as me, only not the same class. She's always getting told off by teachers and she sings really loudly in assembly. She often forgets her coat, but she doesn't seem to notice that it's cold when she's tearing around the playground with the boys.

As more and more pictures of Rose Bedford came into my head, I realized that the new girl couldn't possibly be the one I knew. There's no way the Rose Bedford from *my* school would ever do something like ballet. She wouldn't be able to keep her body still for a start.

Miss Coralie gave her watch a bit of a cross look, then said briskly, "Well, we can't wait any longer." Then, right when no one was expecting it, she suddenly said the magic words, "*Preparation*...and..."

I think it gave Mrs. Marsden a bit of a shock, because her hands flew to the piano and her face looked all flustered. She was only just in time with the *plié* music.

"...*one* and *two* and *rise* and *lower*..." went on Miss Coralie. She always counted and talked in the rhythm of the music. "And *turnout more* and *arm* and *head* and *again* and *two* and *three* and *four* and..."

My legs felt very strong, and I concentrated with all my might on turning out well and not rolling my feet. I couldn't tell if Miss Coralie had noticed my *pliés* yet, because she was behind me, but when we turned to face the other way I could see that she was watching Immy Pearson and Lottie Carroll. Immy and Lottie are really good at ballet. It was obvious that Miss Coralie was going to let *them* do the exam, because her head was tipped to one side. She always does that when she thinks someone's doing well.

As she walked along the *barre* and drew nearer to me, I pulled my tummy in even tighter and turned my legs out as far as they would go. We were doing the *pliés* facing the other way now.

"And *one* and *two* and *very* nice, *Poppy*, and *five* and *six* and *seven* and *eight*."

The inside of my body started zinging. I was so happy. Miss Coralie had said my name before anyone else's. I tried with all my might not to let my face have a showing-off look on it, because I always hate that look when I see it on other girls' faces.

"*Battements tendus*," said Miss Coralie. (All the names of the exercises are in French. That one sounds like *batter mon tarn due*!)

"*Preparation* and..."

When the music started, I felt as though I could do anything. My feet were pointed, my knees were pulled up tight. "Good, Jasmine..."

That made me even happier. Jasmine and I were the only two in the whole class to have been mentioned so far. I don't know if I stopped concentrating for a second because I was so happy but, next thing I knew, Miss Coralie was moving my arm and then my hand. "You look like a wooden soldier, Poppy. Curve it gently..." I really tried to make it curve, but I knew it wasn't working. Miss Coralie got hold of my hand and flapped my arm. "What's this old chicken wing? Hmm?"

I heard a little snigger from behind me and tried to stop my face going pink. Then I lifted my elbow and dropped my shoulder and... "*Lovely*, Poppy, *three* and *four* and..."

Phew!

⁂

By the end of the *barre* work, I felt really tired because I'd been focusing so hard on trying to get everything exactly right. I'm never normally tired in ballet lessons. In fact, the only time I ever feel tired in my whole life is in the morning when Mum wakes me up!

For the centre work, away from the *barre*, we always stand in rows. Miss Coralie tells you which row she wants you in. She put me in the third one, and Jasmine in the second. First we did *port de bras*, which are the arm movements. This is my favourite bit of the whole lesson. The music reminds me of slow motion skiing on silver snow with a golden sky.

I was in my own little world, so it gave me a shock when the door suddenly opened. It's such an unusual thing to happen in the middle of a class that we all stopped what we were doing to turn round and stare. Even Mrs. Marsden stopped playing the piano.

"Ah, Rose," said Miss Coralie.

3 Please Let it Be Me

I nearly gasped out loud. It *was* the Rose Bedford from my school. Only you could hardly recognize her with her hair all scraped back under her hairband. The trouble was, she'd got the hairband too far forwards, so it pressed her eyebrows downwards. And that made her look as though she was really scowling. Her leotard was all wrinkly around her tummy because it was too big for her, and her legs looked strange too, but I couldn't think why that was at first.

I looked at Jasmine to see what she was thinking and realized straight away what was wrong with Rose's legs. It was the way she was standing, with her knees locked right back, and her feet pointing straight ahead, which is the very last way you're supposed to stand when you do ballet. Two girls in the row behind me were smiling like mad and nearly giggling. Everyone else just seemed to be staring.

It felt like ages before Miss Coralie spoke, but it must have only been about two seconds really. "Hello, Rose. We have actually started."

Rose just nodded and took a couple of steps forward.

Miss Coralie used her brisk voice. "Is your mother with you?"

"She's gone now. Her car was on a double yellow, you see."

Miss Coralie smiled then. "Oh, I see. Is that why you're late? Did your mother have trouble parking?"

"Not really – it just took ages to do my hair and everything."

I was surprised when Rose said that. It didn't look as though she'd brushed her hair at all. She'd got nobbly bits sticking out of the top.

Miss Coralie's eyes widened. "Right. Well, let's get on, now you're here," she said rather snappily. "Pop yourself in the third row, Rose. Next to Poppy Vernon."

I moved along a bit to leave a space and that's when Rose noticed me.

"Hiya!" She grinned.

"Hi," I said in a whisper.

"Do you know Poppy, Rose?" asked Miss Coralie.

I could feel everyone's eyes on me now.

"She goes to my school," said Rose, bending her knees and pulling at the bottom of her leotard.

Someone did a little smirky noise behind me and I felt a bit sorry for Rose because it was obvious her pants were uncomfortable and she was trying to put them straight.

"What?" said Rose, turning round and giving the girl behind a cross look.

"Nothing," said the girl quickly.

"Can we get on, please?" said Miss Coralie, her eyes flashing. "Rose, I know you haven't done ballet before, but in your audition I had the feeling that you could be very good if you work hard. That's the only reason I let you come into this class. So you need to concentrate really hard from now on. We don't have talking in class because there isn't time for it. Just keep an eye on me or one of the girls in front of you, and you'll start to pick things up. It'll take quite some time and, as I told you before, you'll have to do some practice at home. All right?"

Rose nodded, but I could tell that she wasn't really listening. She was staring round the room and still fiddling with the bottom of her leotard.

The silver-snow music didn't sound so magical after that, and I didn't do the rest of the *port de bras* as well as usual because I kept on wondering what Rose was doing. When we turned to face the corner, I could see her shoulders all stiff and her legs a bit bent. Miss Coralie didn't correct her at all because she was watching the rest of us so carefully.

Next it was the *adage*, which you pronounce *add-arge*. You have to have good balance for this section. Miss Coralie was going through the step with her back to us, so we could see exactly which leg we were supposed to use, when Rose suddenly started whizzing her arms round really fast like a windmill.

"I'm really stiff from all that slow stuff," she whispered to me.

"You're not supposed to talk," I mouthed back.

Miss Coralie turned round at that moment and frowned at me. "Are you watching, Poppy?"

I nodded hard and tried not to go red. Inside my head, cross thoughts started jabbing and stabbing away, stopping me from concentrating properly. It wasn't fair.

"Facing me...fifth position *croisé*... And..." Miss Coralie didn't count this time. Just watched us hard. "I can't see your face, Sophie. Lovely, Lottie. Tighten the supporting knee, Poppy."

Rose turned round to look at my knee. Then she turned back and stuck her leg up really high at the back, only with a bent supporting leg and her shoulders all stiff. Miss Coralie corrected her and told her how to work at her *arabesques* at home. But I couldn't imagine Rose ever practising at home. It just didn't seem like a Rose thing to do.

After the *adage* section, we moved on to the jumps.

"I'm looking for pointed toes and no bending forwards!" said Miss Coralie briskly.

"Oh, goody," said Rose.

One or two girls giggled, while Immy Pearson gave me a look as if to say: *Haven't you got a weird friend?*

I wasn't sure whether to give her the same look back, so I just looked the other way.

We did lots of jumps, but I don't think I did them very well. The problem was that I could still see Rose out of the corner of my eye. She was putting me off by jumping really high. Her toes were pointed and her knees were straight but she wasn't keeping her arms in the right position or anything. She was just trying to bounce as high as she could. I tried to make myself concentrate, but it was no good.

It was really strange that Rose had come to The Coralie Charlton School of Ballet at all. I couldn't work out why she didn't go to a modern class somewhere. I wondered if I'd dare to ask her afterwards, but I didn't *really* want to talk to her because I kept remembering how scary she was at school, playing with boys and getting told off all the time.

She didn't fit in at Miss Coralie's though.

And I know it's horrible of me, but I didn't want her here either.

After the jumps, it was the most difficult bit of the whole class. The steps. First we do the set steps, but after that Miss Coralie makes up a whole string of steps and puts them together in a sequence. It's supposed to be good training for when we're older. She gives us a new sequence of steps every two weeks. The first week, we learn the sequence and the second week we "polish it up" as she calls it.

I'm terrible at remembering a whole sequence of steps by myself. Usually it doesn't matter, because I just go home and practise like mad. Then at least I'm quite good by the time it's the next lesson. But today was different. Today I wanted to get it right straight away. The biggest jitters of all went whizzing round my body because I knew that, to get picked for the exam, you have to be good at every single part of the lesson. I was glad Jasmine was in the row in front, so I could copy her.

Miss Coralie told us the steps slowly and carefully and I really tried my double best to remember them all. But while she was reeling off the long list of French words, all I could hear was Rose making little noises beside me. "Uh? Wah?"

"Right, I'm going to give you a minute to try out the whole sequence on your own, while I have a quick word with Mrs. Marsden. Then we'll do it properly with the music. Rose, just do the best you can by copying the others."

A minute! That wasn't very long. I knew I had to work fast.

But Rose was hissing in my ear. "What's she on about? Can you show me?"

"Actually, can you copy someone else?" I whispered back. "I'm not much good at steps."

After that, I didn't have time to see what Rose was doing. I was concentrating too hard on learning the sequence myself. Jasmine was working it out right in front of me, so I just kept my eye on her and tried to follow everything she did.

"See, you *are* good at it!" Rose whispered. She was giving me a big friendly smile. "How you do that jumping thing where you have to cross your feet over."

I really wished she'd leave me alone because I hadn't learned it properly yet.

"Right, everyone. Let's try it with the music. We'll start with the back row for a change."

My heart thumped and the jitters started to make me feel sick. We were doing it a row at a time. There was no way I'd be able to do it without Jasmine or at least *someone* to copy.

"And *one* and *two* and *three* and *four*..."

The back row was really good. No wonder, they'd got Immy and Lottie.

"Hey, they're better than us, aren't they?" said Rose.

I nodded miserably.

"Well done, the back row! Now let's have the third row, please."

Jasmine gave me a thumbs-up as I walked on shaky legs to my place.

"And..."

I thought I'd be able to do the first part at least, but even that went wrong. It was because I could see Rose out of the corner of my eye and I knew she was trying to copy me, but she just looked like a grasshopper. And, as soon as I'd had that thought it really put me off. Then I heard Tamsyn giggling and I wasn't sure if it was because of me or because of Rose. It was all right for Rose. She didn't care. She wouldn't be doing the exam anyway. But it was very important for me and now I'd completely messed it up *and* I'd gone red.

Watching Jasmine's row and the front row made me even more miserable, because nearly everyone was better than me. I just had to hope that I'd done the *barre* work and the arms well enough to make up for the steps.

After the *révérence*, Miss Coralie said she was going to tell us who she'd chosen to do the exam. Everyone went to the front, but Jasmine and I stayed near the back of the group. Rose didn't even bother to listen at all. She just wandered over to the *barre* and put her right leg up on it. Miss Coralie didn't seem to mind. It was the end of the lesson, after all.

My heart was beating so hard it was making my top half go quivery. *Please let it be me... Please let it be me... Please let it be me...*

"Now, some of you might be disappointed not to be picked but, as you know, the more advanced you are at ballet, the harder it becomes, and I never let anyone go in for an exam unless I'm quite sure that they'll get a good result."

Everyone nodded and waited. My heart was thumping.

"There's going to be an extra class on Fridays for those people doing the exam, because once a week won't be enough..."

I stood as still as a statue waiting to hear who'd been chosen. But Jasmine was nudging me and jerking her head. She wanted me to look over at the *barre*. When I saw what Rose had done, I nearly gasped out loud. She was facing the *barre* standing on her left leg with the foot turned out. She'd slid her right ankle so far along the *barre* that she was almost in a kind of sideways splits. Even Tamsyn Waters wouldn't be able to do that. It was incredible.

"So these are the people who will be doing the exam this term..."

My eyes shot back to Miss Coralie.

"...and if you're not on the list, it simply means that you'll be doing it next term or whenever you're ready for it. It *doesn't* mean you're no good at ballet, or anything like that, because you're *all* good in this class."

She gave us a quick smile, then her eyes went down to her piece of paper and my eyes went down to the floor.

"Lottie Carroll, Immy Pearson..." I saw them clutch each other and do a little jump of happiness. "...Tamsyn Waters, Sophie James, Isobel Brooks and Jasmine Ayed."

The floor seemed to have gone all blurry. I didn't feel like looking up. Not ever again. Jasmine's arm went round my shoulder. I knew she was only being kind, but I felt like shaking her off because I didn't want her arm round me. My throat was hurting and I was scared that tears were going to come into my eyes. If only I could run away and find a dark little place where I could cry and cry, and nobody would know how heavy all my sadness felt.

Inside my head, a voice was saying: *It's all Rose's fault. She put you off.*

But then I suddenly realized something.

Miss Coralie had read the names off a list. That meant she'd already decided who was going to do the exam before the lesson had even started. So I couldn't blame it on Rose. It was just me. I wasn't good enough. I simply wasn't good enough.

4 Balancing Tears

"Guess what I've made? Tuna pasta!" said Mum.

She was using her bright sparkly voice. The one she'd been using ever since Jasmine and I had got into the car and I'd told her I wasn't doing the exam.

"Never mind," she'd said. "Miss Coralie knows best."

After that, I'd sunk down into the front seat and not said a single word because I was just too sad. It didn't matter though because Mum was doing enough talking for about ten people.

"Do you like tuna pasta, Jasmine?" she said,

lifting her chin so that her eyes could look in the driving mirror.

"Yes, lovely," said Jasmine in a quiet voice. *She'd* been using her quiet voice ever since we'd left class.

"We're just going to pick up Stevie from Mark Mason's..."

That made me talk. "Oh, no! Mum, you said you weren't picking up Stevie till later!"

"Well, Mark's mum and dad have got to go out and they want to make sure Mark's ready for bed before the baby-sitter arrives, so I said we'd pick Stevie up early."

"Oh, Mum! He'll only pester me and Jasmine all the time."

"No, he won't because I won't let him," said Mum, still in her bright voice. Then she suddenly sounded a bit tired. "Let's put some music on, shall we?"

I think she was fed up of talking. She was probably fed up of me, too. But I couldn't help being in such a bad mood. This was the worst day of my life, and now it was even worse because I was going to have to put up with my little brother hanging around when I'd got Jasmine for tea.

I sighed a great big silent sigh that made my shoulders go right up and back down again, then I sank even lower into my seat. It was going to be horrible next term with Jasmine in a different class and me stuck with Rose Bedford and her grasshopper jumps and silly grunty noises. If it hadn't been for her, I would have done the step sequence much better, and then I might…

But I couldn't blame Rose, could I? All I could do was sit there with a big lump in my throat, listening to Mum's CD.

No one said another word till we got to Mark Mason's.

"You two stay here. I won't be a minute."

As soon as Mum had got out of the car,

Jasmine leaned forwards. "Hey, Poppy, Miss Coralie might change her mind, you know… If you practise like mad and I help you with the steps… And we could tell her that it was Rose putting you off…"

"But it wasn't just because of Rose…"

"Yes it was! You're normally *much* better than you were today."

"I wish she'd never joined our class. She made me do everything wrong."

"I know. It's not fair, is it? Does she act like that at school as well?"

"She's always playing with the boys and forever getting told off. I don't know why she's coming to ballet."

"Maybe her mum *made* her."

I nodded miserably.

"But if you really *really* practise the sequence like mad and next week we tell Miss Coralie that you couldn't concentrate properly because of Rose…"

"I'm not sure..."

At that moment, the back door was yanked open and my little brother got in the car.

"Hey, Mark's got a baseball cap with a light on it and he can even read in the dark, only it wasn't dark so we couldn't really test it out."

I didn't say anything. I didn't even turn round. My throat was hurting again. I just wanted to get home and go up to my room and carry on talking with Jasmine. I was glad she thought it was Rose's fault though, and not mine. That made me feel a teensy bit better.

"So you had a good time then, Stevie," laughed Mum, doing up her seat belt.

"Yeah, wicked!"

I don't know if Stevie suddenly realized that I was being a bit quiet, but he leaned right forwards and peered round at my face. "Why is Poppy balancing tears, Mum?"

I stayed very still and tried really hard not to

let any fall but it didn't work, so then my throat was in agony because of trying not to make any crying noises.

"Seat belt, Stevie. Now!" said Mum.

Stevie made Jasmine play thumb war with him for the rest of the way home, so I didn't have to speak, thank goodness. I could feel Mum looking sideways at me though. I managed to blink my tears away when she wasn't looking and then I concentrated hard on what Jasmine had said. Maybe she was right. Perhaps Miss Coralie *would* change her mind.

While Mum was getting the tea ready, Jasmine and I stayed up in my room.

"I don't know what Papa's going to say," said Jasmine.

"Your *dad*?"

She nodded. "You know he hates ballet."

"Yes, but he lets you do it, doesn't he?"

"He doesn't mind at the moment, because

he's no idea how much practice I do and how much I love it."

"Will he be cross that you're doing the exam?"

"He might not let me do the extra lessons – then *I* won't be able to do the exam either."

"Oh no!" I felt so sorry for poor Jasmine. "Couldn't you ask your mum not to tell him?"

Jasmine's eyes went massive as she shook her head.

I knew as soon as I said it that it was a silly idea. Jasmine's dad's quite scary. Jasmine's told me that she's only allowed to carry on with ballet until she's eleven and then her dad wants her to concentrate on school work and the piano.

"You're not eleven for ages, Jasmine. So surely your dad won't mind."

She did a big sigh. "I'll have to make sure he doesn't realize how much ballet practice I'm doing. Otherwise, he'll only start going on about how I'm neglecting my school work and how unnatural it is to do all that stretching and turning out and everything."

"It's better than turning *in.*" I knew I was sounding a bit stroppy, but I couldn't help it. I'd made myself remember Rose again. "I felt quite sorry for Rose Bedford at first, but I don't now. I wish Miss Coralie had made her stand next to someone who was good at steps, then it wouldn't have mattered if she'd kept pestering them."

"Never mind her. Let's try out the new steps," said Jasmine, jumping up.

But before you could say *sequence*, my door was pushed open and Stevie stood there looking rather guilty. "It's teatime."

"Have you been listening outside my bedroom door, Stevie?"

"I only heard the bit about Rose Bedford. What did she do?"

"Nothing," I said. But Jasmine had spoken at the same time.

"She put Poppy off and now Poppy can't do the exam."

Stevie wasn't even listening. "She's cool, she is!"

Jasmine gave him a puzzled look. "What do you mean?"

I put on a bit of a sneery voice. "Stevie thinks anyone who plays with Archie Cook is cool."

"Who's Archie Cook?"

"Only the best footballer in the whole school!" said Stevie. "He lets me join in sometimes. He says I'm quite good for a year two."

"Come on, you lot. It'll go cold!" came Mum's voice from downstairs.

The moment my brother had raced off, Jasmine put her arm round me. "We'll work on the new sequence after tea, shall we?"

"Okay, but I don't think it'll make any difference," I said in a glum voice.

"Yes, it will!" said Jasmine. Then she stuck her

thumb up in the air. "Come on!" I put my thumb against hers, closed my eyes and made my silent wish.

Please let Miss Coralie change her mind next week.

5 Is It All a Trick?

The next morning at school was good fun because in literacy hour we were listening to music to help us with creative writing. Miss Morrison played my very favourite piece of music in the whole world – *Waltz of the Flowers* from *The Nutcracker Suite*. I was the last one out to play after the lesson because I wanted to finish off what I was writing. I'd only just gone out of the year-five door, when I saw Rose Bedford with Tom Priest and Archie Cook.

It gave me a bit of a shock when Rose started talking to me as though we were best friends.

"Hi. I've been waiting ages. I thought you must be away."

Tom Priest was grinning in a horrible way. "Do you do ballet?" he said to me.

I tried to sound not bothered. "Yeah. So what?"

Archie Cook put his arms up into fifth position – at least, what *he* thought fifth position was – and started turning round on tiptoe like one of those little ballet dancers in a musical box.

I didn't say anything, just started to walk away.

"They're being silly. Take no notice," said Rose.

I kept walking because I didn't want to talk to Rose.

But she was following me. "Were you fed up that you weren't chosen for the exam?" she asked.

I felt like turning round and snapping: *It's all your fault, you know!* But I didn't dare, so I just shook my head and walked a bit faster. I could see my friends, Mia and Alice, on the other side of the playground.

Rose was talking again. "I'm giving up at the end of term. I don't like it."

That made me turn round. "Why are you doing it then?"

"My mum's making me because Granny gave it to me for my birthday."

"What do you mean?"

"My present was one term's ballet lessons, even though she knew I'd absolutely hate it."

"Why did she give you ballet lessons if she knew that you don't like ballet?"

"I think she wants me to stop being a tomboy and start wearing skirts more and things like that."

At our school, girls are allowed to wear trousers. I couldn't imagine Rose ever wearing a skirt, even if she did ballet for a hundred years.

"So you're definitely giving it up?" I knew it

was horrible of me, but I wanted to be sure I wasn't going to have to put up with her for any longer than one term.

"Yeah." She suddenly did one of the kind of jumps where you have to beat your feet in the air. "Is this right?"

It wasn't, but I nodded anyway. Then I turned, because Mia and Alice were waving to tell me to come over.

Rose grabbed my arm. "Can you show me how to do it properly, Poppy?"

I didn't really want to, but I thought that maybe, if I just showed her quickly, she'd leave me alone.

"You start like this, okay?" She copied my third position quite well. "Then you bend your knees out to the side..."

A big snorty noise from the other side of the playground made Rose and I turn round at exactly the same moment.

Archie and Tom were by the drinking

fountain pointing at me, and laughing.

"Shut up, you two!" called Rose. But, when she turned back, I saw that she was grinning like mad. "Yeah, what do you do next?"

I suddenly realized I'd still got my legs bent in a *plié*, which must have looked totally stupid. A terrible thought came into my head. *I bet Rose tricked me into showing her the beats specially so her friends could make fun of me.*

At that moment, I hated Rose Bedford. I really did.

6 Making the Air Swirl

On Saturday afternoon I went to Jasmine's house. Her dad was out. I was glad he wasn't there, because he's so scary. It's not just ballet he's strict about, it's things like playing with friends and watching television.

Jasmine's mum's not half as strict. I expect she guessed that Jasmine and I would be practising ballet up in Jasmine's room, but she just said, "I'm sorry you are down in the dumps about the exam, Poppy." I liked the way Jasmine's mum sounded, all gentle. She's got a lovely accent because she's French.

As soon as we were on our own, I asked Jasmine if her dad minded the extra class.

"He's a bit annoyed about it, but I'm allowed to do it, thank goodness."

"Hey, that's brill, Jazz! Did you start the exam dance?"

Her eyes sparkled. "Yes! That's why I asked Maman if you could come round. You see, I thought I could teach you the part we learned so you'll really know it well when Miss Coralie starts teaching the whole class on Tuesday. Then she'll definitely change her mind about the exam!"

Jasmine's bedroom is much bigger than mine, but we made it even bigger by clearing everything off the floor and putting her beanbag on the bed. We changed into our ballet things and did a proper warm-up so we wouldn't strain any muscles. Then we spent ages and ages making sure I could do every single step of the dance perfectly.

"Right," said Jasmine. "Now for the sequence."

So then we worked on *that* too. But we didn't just go through it normally. We added a few extra bits to make it more interesting.

"Let's put it to music!" Jasmine suddenly said.

"Yesss! *Waltz of the Flowers*!"

We had to change the timing but it was brilliant fun.

"I know it's a funny thing to say, but the air in this room feels different, doesn't it? As though we've made it swirl around because we've been dancing so much." I felt a bit stupid saying it, but it was what I felt inside.

Jasmine nodded and danced her fingers through the air as though she was testing it out. Then she stopped and said, "Shall we ask Maman to come and watch?"

At that moment, there was a knock at the door.

"Great, she's here!" said Jasmine, pulling

open the door. "Maman, do you want..."

It wasn't Jasmine's mum, though. It was her dad. A big smile covered his whole face. But when he saw that I was there, and that both of us were wearing our ballet leotards, the smile started to slide away.

"Hello, Papa!" said Jasmine, giving him a hug.

"Hello, Doctor Ayed," I said. Only my voice didn't come out properly because I was nervous, so it sounded like: "Hell Doc Ay".

"And what are you two doing?"

"Just...dancing..." said Jasmine. She sounded as nervous as *I* felt.

It must feel really strange to be scared of your dad, like Jasmine is. I'm glad I'm not afraid of mine.

"I can see that. But what, exactly?"

"Just making up a dance for fun, that's all."

Doctor Ayed frowned as though Jasmine had said something in a strange foreign language.

"Hm..." Then he gave her what I call a *thin lips* smile. It's the sort of smile that grown-ups give you when they've got some cross things to say but they're saving it up for later. "I think tea will be ready soon."

When he'd gone, the air stopped swirling around and stayed quite still. So we sat on Jasmine's bed and I told her about Rose.

"I could tell she only got me to show her the jumps to make the boys laugh, Jazz."

"That was mean of her."

"I know. But I got her back, because when she tried to sit on my table at lunchtime I made sure there wasn't a space anywhere near."

"Good. That showed *her*!"

"I know. And the next day she started talking to me in the playground, but Tom and Archie were with her so I didn't even reply. I think she knows I don't want to be friends now, because today she didn't come anywhere near me."

"At least that means she'll definitely leave

you alone at ballet next week."

I couldn't help feeling a little judder of excitement. But it only lasted for about a second, then my body went all floppy like a wet tea towel. "It won't make any difference."

"Yes, it will!" said Jasmine, linking her arm with mine. "We're going to get Miss Coralie to change her mind, and that's that!"

"Do you really *really* think she might?"

"Course I do."

And this time I got a little tickle of excitement that didn't turn into a wet-towel feeling, but grew into a lovely big burst of sunshiny hope.

7 Trapped in the Circle

On Tuesday, I got more and more excited as the day went on. I'm always like this on Tuesdays, because it's ballet after school. I wish it could be ballet after school every single day. But *this* Tuesday was especially important. I had christened it Last-Chance Tuesday.

At morning break, I rushed outside with Mia and Alice, but stopped when I heard Rose's voice behind me.

"Hey, Poppy..."

"What?" I asked, turning round.

I got quite a shock. She was standing very

straight with her hair scraped right back and not a bump in sight. On her face was a proud grin.

"Thought I'd get myself all ready today, then I won't be late! Look!" She turned round and I saw that she'd even twizzled her ponytail into a bun and gripped it in place.

I didn't know what to say. The trouble was, if I acted nice and friendly, Rose would only start talking in the middle of ballet, and it would be absolutely terrible if she put me off again. So I just said, "Oh yeah," and hoped she'd go away.

But she didn't. And to make everything double bad, a group of grinning boys suddenly appeared. They made a circle round us and I felt a bit scared standing in the middle with Rose.

"Ro's getting girlie!" chanted Tom and Archie. "Ro's getting girlie!"

"I am *not*!" screeched Rose, sticking her neck out and nearly spitting, she was so cross. "Get lost, you lot!"

But they didn't.

I really wanted to escape and leave Rose to sort the boys out, but something was stopping me. It was a funny thought to be thinking, but Rose with a neat bun seemed like a different girl from tomboy Rose. And I would have felt horrible leaving this new Rose with all those nasty boys.

"Talking to your little ballet friend?" asked Alex in a high-pitched voice.

"With your little bunny-bun-bun!" said Tom.

The other boys just laughed and started going round on tiptoe with bent legs and high arms, because that's the only ballet step boys know.

"Rosie Posie does ballet! Rosie Posie's getting girlie!" they all chanted.

"I am *not*! And don't call me that!" yelled Rose.

That only made them chant louder. "Rosie Posie! Rosie Posie!"

I could tell she was getting really furious,

staring at the boys as though she would burst with anger. Then she suddenly reached round to the back of her head and started tugging. One or two hairgrips fell to the ground. Next she ripped the elastic band off her ponytail. It must have really hurt her because she did it so roughly. She shook her head hard a few times, and her hair fell round her shoulders, so she was back to normal.

The boys stopped going round and round and stared at her.

She stared right back, with black eyes flashing in an angry white face, and spoke in a sneery voice. "Did someone switch off the music box?"

Then she punched Tom on the arm and, while he was clutching it, pushed her way past him and ran away laughing.

"I'll get you back, Ro! You wait!"

Tom roared after Rose and I was left standing there.

Archie Cook pointed at my face and started a new chant. "Poppy is pathetic!" Then the others joined in. "Poppy is pathetic! Poppy is pathetic!"

"I am *not*!" I said, trying to sound strong and stroppy like Rose had done. But it didn't work.

A boy called Dillon started sneering. "Why d'you do ballet then?"

"Yeah, why d'you do it?" said Archie, laughing.

I took a deep breath to try and make my voice come out louder. "I'm not the only one," I said.

"Hey, Ro's told me what the teacher's called," said Dillon, grinning round the circle. "Miss Coralie!"

Archie started pointing his toes in a really silly way and saying, "Ooh-hoo, look at me, Miss Coralie!"

I could feel my heart beating near my throat. That probably meant that I was going to cry in a minute, so I knew I had to get out of the circle at once. If only Mia and Alice would come over and save me. I could see them talking to the teacher in the far corner of the playground. She was smiling and nodding at them.

I pressed my thumbs together hard.

Please look over in this direction. Please look over in this direction.

But they didn't.

Archie started jumping from foot to foot, pointing his toes in a really clumsy way. I couldn't bear it for a second longer. I'd just have to act like Rose for once. That was the only way I was ever going to get away. Before I could change my mind, I gave Archie a big shove on the chest and called out some words that I'd heard once on telly. "Shut up, skank brain!"

It gave me a shock when he lost his balance and fell over. "Yowwwch! You've made me break my wrist now!" he screeched.

The boys all went quiet then and one of them bent down beside Archie. "You all right?"

Archie just clutched his wrist tightly and made little grunting noises as he stared at it with his face all screwed up. I wished I could go back in time and undo my big shove.

"What's going on here!"

Mrs. Appleton was striding over looking furious. Now I felt as though someone was trying to squeeze the air out of me.

"Poppy pushed Archie over," said Dillon, giving me a horrible look.

"Sorry," I said. But I didn't have any spit in my mouth because of being so worried and my *sorry* came out as a teeny little whisper.

Mrs. Appleton was bending down beside Archie, speaking in a soothing voice.

"Just try moving it very gently, dear. That's right. Does it hurt when you do that?"

"Aargh!" yelped Archie. "It's agony."

Mrs. Appleton nodded. "Come on, let's get you on your feet... At least it's not broken."

"My back hurts too," said Archie in a really

whiny voice. Then he gave me a horrible scowl. "And my chest..."

Mrs. Appleton suddenly swung round to look at me. "What do you think you're playing at, Poppy? This isn't the way to behave! Imagine what it'd be like if Miss Cherry felt a bit cross with me and decided to push me over! That wouldn't do at all, would it?"

I shook my head and tried to think of something to say that would show Mrs. Appleton I wasn't completely horrible. "Erm... you see...the thing is...Archie said ballet was stupid..."

"Well, I'm sorry, Poppy, but I'm afraid that is absolutely no excuse for knocking him flat! The poor boy's hurt his wrist and has probably got a bit of a bruise on his...lower back."

"It's really painful, Miss," said Archie, clutching his bottom and screwing up his face.

Mrs. Appleton put her arm round his shoulder, told him gently that his wrist definitely wasn't broken, then snapped at me, "What do you say to Archie?"

I caught a glimpse of Stevie by the netting, watching all that was going on.

"Sorry," I whispered for the second time, with a face like a tomato.

"I should think so too. There's far too much of this lashing out at the least provocation these days, and we're not having it in this school. Now off you go, Poppy."

I didn't look at anyone. Just ran to Mia and Alice as fast as my shaky legs would take me.

None of the teachers gave me any bad looks during lunch, so I made myself stop thinking about Archie Cook and his horrid friends and concentrated on ballet instead. It was in the afternoon break that my big jitters started. I decided to go to the cloakroom and have quick practice of the step sequence from the last lesson. I couldn't wait to show Miss Coralie that I could already do it perfectly before she even started to polish up what we'd learned last week.

The first thing I did when I got into the cloakroom was hold on to one of the basins and do a *plié.* I like pretending the basin's a *barre* because it's exactly the right height. I sung the *plié* music very softly and did one facing the other way to make it even.

I was just straightening my legs when I thought I heard a little noise coming from one of the toilets. I looked at the locks on all the five doors. One of them was on red. That meant someone was in there. I felt a bit silly because they must have heard me singing, so I decided to go to the loo myself, then by the time I came out the person would have gone. It was a pity I couldn't go into the classroom to dance, but we're not allowed inside during break unless it's raining.

When I heard one of the loos flushing, I thought *Good, they're going at last!* I counted to twenty, then flushed my own toilet and went back into the cloakroom. No one was there. Thank goodness.

I went through the step sequence four times, then I did the dance. I kept counting all the time, sometimes in my head, sometimes out loud. It helped me get it right. The noise of the end-of-break bell gave me a jump because I'd been so wrapped up in my own little ballet world – my favourite place to be.

Just before I left the cloakroom, I said my little prayer for the sixty-sixth-millionth time… Only this time I said it out loud to make it work better.

"Please let Miss Coralie change her mind about me doing the exam."

8 Goose Bumps

After school, Mum came to collect me and Stevie. She was standing at the gate, as usual, chatting to Mark Mason's mum, so I hung around with Mia, waiting impatiently for her to finish. I didn't want to be even ten seconds late setting off for ballet. I wanted to make sure I had enough time to run through the sequence with Jasmine before the class started.

But I got a shock because when I looked again, Mum wasn't talking to Mark's mum any more. She was talking with Mrs. Appleton. And looking very serious. My heart did a massive yo-

yo and my body went all tense with worry. They had to be talking about me and Archie. Mum was going to be really cross. I could just imagine her telling me off all the way home. That was the trouble with adults. They were the only ones who were allowed to talk when they were telling you off. And if you dared to interrupt they said you were being cheeky. I'd just have to make sure I said the word *bullying* right at the very beginning, because *that* would make her listen. Once I'd got her to listen, I'd explain about how they were ganging up on me.

"I've got to go. Bye, Mia."

"Come on, Stevie. We're going," Mum called when she saw me walking across to her.

"Byeee, Poppy! See you tomorrow!"

Mia was so lucky. She didn't have to worry about getting told off or having her whole life ruined because of not being chosen for a ballet exam.

The moment we got in the car, Stevie started

telling Mum about football.

"You should have seen me, Mum, I was absolutely wicked! Mr. Palmer said I did really good footwork. When we got back to the classroom, he gave me this sticker! Look! It says I'm a star! See!"

Stevie was leaning forward, tapping Mum on the shoulder.

"Sit down, Stevie, and put your seat belt on. I'll look when we get home."

Uh-oh! Mum didn't sound very happy, and I could easily guess why.

Stevie didn't seem to notice. He was too full of his goal. "Mr. Palmer's written 'football' on the sticker, Mum. Now it says *I'm a football star!* Clever, isn't it!"

Mum's voice reminded me of a pair of nail clippers. "Yes, well done, Stevie. Is your seat belt done up properly?"

"He said I was a dead cert for the first team next year. What *is* a dead cert?"

No answer. I could see the side of Mum's face from where I was sitting. It looked as though the bones were moving in her jaw. She was definitely thinking very cross thoughts.

I was dreading getting home. Half of me wanted to get the telling-off over with right here and now, but the other half thought that if I kept quiet Mum might just forget about it.

The moment we got home, Stevie kicked off his shoes and rushed off to watch cartoons, and I went whizzing off to do my hair and get my ballet things ready. I was halfway up the stairs when Mum's voice stopped me.

"I want a word with you, young lady." Goose bumps came up under my school sweatshirt. "Come into the kitchen."

I shot back down as fast as possible, because I was so anxious about ballet. I couldn't be late on this most important day in the world, and the traffic was always really bad if we were even the teensiest bit late.

"I know what you're going to say, Mum, and it wasn't my fault. Honestly. I double promise. It was Archie big bully Cook and his friends saying nasty stuff about ballet..."

"Hold it right there, Poppy!"

Another coating of goose bumps sprang up all over me.

Mum put her hands on her waist. "Mrs. Appleton has told me the full story, Poppy. You pushed Archie over. Hard. And he hurt himself! I cannot believe that a daughter of mine did that. I don't know what Dad'll say…"

"But… "

"Don't interrupt! It's all too easy to blame the boys, these days. But on this occasion, Poppy, *you* were the bully!"

"I wasn't! It's not fair!"

"Which bit isn't fair? Did you push Archie Cook over or not?"

"Y…yes…but it was because he was making

fun of me." I knew my voice was getting louder but I couldn't help it. "And they made a circle round me and I couldn't get out..."

Mum pressed her hands together and put them in front of her lips, frowning.

"Made a circle?"

I thought that I was making her understand, at last. But then I suddenly caught sight of the clock and my whole body stiffened. "Oh, no! I'm going to be late for ballet. We've got to go right now or I'll get killed! I'll tell you in the car, okay?"

There was no time for another word. I just belted out and pulled the door behind me. Unfortunately, it slammed.

"Come back here!" Mum sounded *really* angry now.

"*Please* can I tell you about it in the car?" I said, poking my head round the kitchen door and trying to sound sensible and grown-up, even though I felt like screaming the place down.

"No, you can't, because you're not going to ballet."

The blood seemed to drain right out of my face and down my neck and my body until I was completely wobbly and weak. "What...?"

"Come in properly and close the door," Mum went on in her icy voice. "I haven't finished talking about what happened today, and you do *not* go racing off when I'm right in the middle of talking to you."

I stood with my head hanging down. This was the worst moment of my life.

"Can I have a sandwich, Mum?"

Stevie had come sliding into the kitchen, which he always does when he's only got socks on his feet. Mum doesn't usually mind, but today she was in too much of a bad mood to put up with it.

"I'll bring you one in a minute. I'm just talking to Poppy."

Stevie stopped sliding and stood with his legs

wide apart. He could tell something was wrong. "What are you talking about?"

I was about to tell him to mind his own business when he suddenly answered his own question. "I bet it's Archie Cook."

I looked up then. Mum was frowning. "What do you know about that?"

"I heard Mrs. Appleton telling you that Archie hurt his wrist..." Stevie was slowly going down into a sort of sideways splits as his feet were sliding further apart. So the next bit of what he said came out as grunts. "Only...he...never did...hurt...it..."

Mum marched over to Stevie and plonked him into a normal standing position. Then she tilted his chin to make him look at her. "Stand still and talk properly."

Stevie did as he was told. "I just saw Archie laughing behind Mrs. Appleton's back, that's all."

"Laughing?"

"Yeah, when Poppy was getting told off."

My eyes widened. I wanted Stevie to keep going, but I could tell he was getting hungry because his eyes kept darting over to the loaf of bread.

"And how do you know that Archie hadn't hurt his wrist?" asked Mum.

"Because he was waving it about, showing off and pulling faces right behind Mrs. Appleton's back when she was being cross with Poppy. Then, the moment she turned round he pretended it was hurting again."

Now Mum's eyes were widening. They looked like big buttons. She didn't seem to be able to speak for a few seconds, but then it was as though someone had bashed her on the back and made the words come shooting out. "Go on then, Poppy, get your stuff, quick. We'll talk in the car."

I could have hugged Stevie, but there was no time. I couldn't waste a single second. I *had* to get to ballet on time.

9 Last Chance

"Calm down, love!"

"I can't calm down. I'm all worried."

All my wishing had come to nothing because here we were, stuck in a great long line of traffic, moving very slowly.

I yanked my leotard and tights out of my bag. "I'm going to get changed right now, Mum."

"People might see your pants," said Stevie, grinning.

"Don't be silly, Stevie. Just calm down, Poppy. I'll come in and explain to Miss Coralie..."

"No. Parents don't come in. Not ever, Mum. You can't."

I wriggled out of my school skirt and managed to get my tights on without undoing the seat belt for more than ten seconds.

"Be good if we had a police siren, wouldn't it?" said Stevie. Then he made the noise of a siren right until I'd got my leotard on.

"Oh, do be quiet, Stevie. I can't drive with all that racket going on."

I felt a bit better because I'd only got my hair to do, but my heart was still beating faster than usual because we were going so slowly.

Mum was making tutting noises and craning her neck out of the car window. "This doesn't look too good."

"What? What?" I felt like crying. I'd just spotted the clock in the front and it said twenty-five past four. The class started at half past.

"Look, Poppy, there's nothing we can do about it, so stop getting yourself in a state."

But I couldn't stop. I *was* in a state. And I was frantically rummaging through my bag, looking for my hairband. It wasn't there.

"Oh, no! I haven't got my hairband! What am I going to do?" And then I *did* burst into tears.

The clock said twenty-eight minutes past four and our car wasn't moving at all.

"Why doesn't the light change to green?" I asked Mum through my tears.

"I'm afraid it's changed already, love," said Mum, doing a big sigh. "There's just so much traffic. It's because we set off that bit later." She turned round and gave me a sorrowful smile. "Put your hair in a bun, love. You've got plenty of grips, haven't you?"

I nodded miserably and started doing what she said.

"Look, we're moving!" said Stevie.

I sat up straight to look, but we only moved about two metres. And when I saw the clock I started going mad, shouting and crying at the same time.

"It's half past. I'm going to be late for definite now. And everyone'll stare and I haven't even got a hairband and that'll make them stare harder... It's no good. I can't go. Let's go home."

"No, we really are moving, now," said Stevie. "Look, it's on green! Go on, Mum, get through it quick!"

And a few seconds later we were in the High Street, but we were still only crawling along.

"Bet Poppy could run faster than this car's going!" said Stevie.

I unclicked my seat belt. "Yes! Can I, Mum?"

"No, it's too far on your own. We'll be there in a minute."

"Oh, pleeeeeease, Mum. You can watch me all the way. I'll leave my bag in the car and just take my ballet shoes. *Pleeeeeease!*"

We'd stopped again and I think that's what

made Mum agree. "Go on, then. I'll see you at the end of the lesson. Bye, darling."

I shot out of the car and ran harder than I've ever run before, feeling silly because of wearing my ballet uniform with my school shoes in the middle of such a busy road.

When I got to the heavy door, I crashed my body against it and it opened so easily that I fell over just inside. It hurt a bit but I just got up and carried on running up the steps. By the time I was at the top, I was completely puffed out. It was the *plié* music, so I'd only missed one thing.

I quickly put on my ballet shoes and noticed that there was a big black mark on my tights. That must have happened when I fell over downstairs. I gulped and rubbed it but it only went smudgy so I left it and chucked my shoes in the changing room, then stood glued to the floor outside Room One...

A little voice inside my head said: *You can't go in looking like that, Poppy.* But another fierce little voice said: *Just go, Poppy!* Before I could change my mind, I pressed my thumbs together, then took a deep breath and pushed open the door.

I didn't look at anyone. Just said, "Sorry I'm late," in a bit of a squeaky voice and went over to Jasmine. Her eyes were full of questions as she bunched up closer to Immy Pearson to make room for me. I knew everyone was staring at me, so I couldn't say anything, and anyway, Miss Coralie wanted to get on.

"*Battements tendus... Preparation...*and..."

I caught sight of myself in one of the mirrors and wished I could disappear into thin air. I looked such a mess. My face was bright red. It was obvious I'd been crying and my bun was nearly falling out. Then there was that awful black mark on my tights.

Miss Coralie was using her no-nonsense counting voice, moving along the line with her straightest back and sternest face. When she got to me, she lifted my arm up. "No hairband, Poppy?"

"We were in a big hurry," I whispered, trying to keep my turnout and my *pointe*.

"Hmm."

She moved on to Jasmine and then to Lottie, all the time counting in a louder voice than usual. My heart was still thudding from running so hard, but now it was thudding from nervousness too.

It wasn't till we were over halfway through the *barre* work that I felt normal again. I had a quick glance around and saw that no one was looking at me any more, thank goodness. Right, from now on I was going to concentrate like mad and not let anything put me off. Especially Rose Bedford.

I suddenly realized that I'd completely forgotten about Rose until now. She was on the *barre* on the opposite wall with her hair looking bobbly and bumpy again, her hairband pressing her eyebrows down and her big leotard in wrinkles all over her tummy. There was *something* different about her though, only I couldn't work out what.

"And *one* and *close* and *second* and *close*, derri*ère* and *close* and *sec*ond and *close*..." said Miss Coralie, walking slowly around, watching everyone with her eagle eye. "And *one* and *two* and *use* your *heads*, don't *roll* your *feet* and *straigh*ten knees." The music came to an end, but Miss Coralie wanted to do the whole exercise again. "A lot of you are gripping the *barre* far too tightly," she said. "Come a step away, and we'll try it without holding on at all."

I glanced at Rose. She had already taken a step away from the *barre* and had prepared her arms and everything. It was really strange. She seemed to be trying so hard, considering she hated ballet. And that reminded me of how she'd put her hair in a neat bun at school, even though she must have known the boys would tease her about it. I didn't understand Rose. She was a mystery girl.

"Concentrate, Poppy," came Miss Coralie's voice, and I realized I'd slipped into a daydream. Immediately, I told myself off.

You stupid thing, Poppy! Then I made a promise inside my head that from now on I would do my double best every single second of the rest of the lesson.

When it was the *ronds de jambe,* Miss Coralie actually tipped her head on one side and said, "Lovely, Poppy."

I wanted to skip around the room shouting, "Yesssssss!" But I made myself stay completely still as though I hadn't even heard her.

Then it was time for the centre work.

"Right, let's have the same rows as last week, but all move forward one row, and the front row from last week go to the back."

"Excuse me, Miss Coralie?" It was Rose who had spoken. Everyone stared at her because it's so unusual to hear anyone's voice except Miss Coralie's in ballet lessons. "Can I change rows, please?"

Miss Coralie looked a bit puzzled. "Change rows? Why?"

"Er...because I was wondering if I could go on the back row today."

"Why?"

"So that I can copy better, because there'll be more people in front of me, you see."

Everyone waited to see what Miss Coralie would say.

"It'll mess up the numbers if I put you in the back row, Rose..."

"I could swap with someone..."

A sort of mask of crossness came over Miss Coralie's face because of Rose arguing. "Just stay where you were last week, next to Poppy. Thank you, Rose."

So Rose stood next to me, but she didn't look very happy. It was no wonder, really. After all, I hadn't exactly been friendly with her at school.

When we did the *port de bras*, Miss Coralie had to tell Rose to stop squashing Sophie, who was on the other side of her, and to stand a bit closer to me. I started wondering whether I smelled horrible or something then, because surely Rose wouldn't care about having to stand next to me all *that* much.

I got another "lovely" from Miss Coralie for my *port de bras*, which gave me the crazy *yesssssss!* feeling, but still I didn't let it show. Then my heart started pounding with excitement as I thought, *Just wait till you see how well I can do the step sequence, then!*

We did lots of beats after the *adage* and, during this part of the lesson, Miss Coralie had to tell Rose to move up again because she was nearly jumping on Sophie's toes. Next, we did the ordinary steps and I saw from the clock on the wall that there wasn't much time left. I wished we could hurry up and get on with the step sequence that I'd practised. *And* the dance.

"Now," said Miss Coralie, "this week, for a change, we're not going to do any polishing work on last week's sequence. Instead, I'm going to teach you another brand new set of steps because I think we need more practice at learning sequences at speed."

My heart sank down to the elastic on my ballet shoes, and Jasmine turned round and gave me a worried look. I very nearly blurted out, *Please can we do the one we did last week first?* but just managed to stop myself in time. Miss Coralie wouldn't have been at all pleased if I'd tried to interfere with what she'd planned.

The sequence seemed even more complicated than last week's. While Miss Coralie was showing us all the steps, my eyes started to water from concentrating so hard on her feet, trying to remember when it should be left in front and when right, when to face the left corner and when to face the right.

"Mark it through, Rose," said Miss Coralie in a slightly puzzled voice.

And that's when I noticed that Rose was standing completely still, staring straight ahead as though she was in a trance. "It's okay, thanks," she said, politely.

But Miss Coralie obviously didn't find it very polite. From the look on her face, you'd think Rose had called her a big fat pig or something. Her voice came out louder than usual. "I'm not asking you, I'm *telling* you."

Rose didn't go at all red, even though lots of people were giving her funny looks. She just started doing as she was told.

A minute later, Miss Coralie clapped her hands quite sharply. I think Rose had put her in a bad mood. "Right, let's try it a row at a time. Front row first."

I watched Jasmine carefully, my mind racing away trying to remember everything.

"Not a bad attempt, front row. Second row, please."

This was it. I took a deep breath and got ready to focus.

"And..."

I tried my very hardest, but it was nearly as bad as last week. I could have burst into tears, because everything was going wrong.

We spent about five more minutes trying to improve the sequence, then Miss Coralie said that there wasn't time to start learning the dance. "Never mind, girls, we'll start it next week. Let's do the curtsey to finish."

I wished I could sink down through the floor and go on sinking down and down in the dark and stay there for ever. My last chance had gone now. Really really gone.

10 Friends

After the curtsey, Jasmine raised her eyebrows at me. She meant: *Wait till everyone's gone so we can talk to Miss Coralie.*

I did a teeny little shake of my head.

"Why not?" she hissed.

I whispered right in her ear. "There's no point."

"But what about the dance...?"

I shook my head again because I was just too sad to speak, and started walking away. Everyone else had gone out except Rose, who was dipping her foot into the rosin tray at the back of the room. If Miss Coralie saw her she'd be really cross because you're not supposed to touch the rosin. It's for the older girls to give their ballet shoes extra grip when they're standing on *pointe.*

"Excuse me, Miss Coralie," said Jasmine.

I got a shock because I knew she was going to say something about me and I was certain Miss Coralie wouldn't even have time to listen. She was wearing a big frown, working out a step with her hands.

"Yes, Jasmine."

Jasmine was using her politest voice. "I was wondering if you could possibly watch Poppy doing the dance."

I felt myself going red.

"I haven't time, I'm afraid, Jasmine. I'm starting the next class in a second." She wasn't even listening.

I opened the door, wanting to get away before any embarrassing tears started dripping down my face.

Then something surprising happened. Rose suddenly rushed up to Miss Coralie, gabbling away loudly. "It was *my* fault that Poppy didn't do her best last week. You see, I put her off by standing right next to her and asking her to help me."

I stared at Rose, open-mouthed. Miss Coralie stopped what she was doing and looked a bit shocked.

"Her brother told me in the playground. He said that he'd been ear-wigging at Poppy's bedroom door and he'd heard her talking to Jasmine."

Now Miss Coralie looked bewildered. "What *are* you talking about, Rose?"

"I'm talking about how I've been trying to keep away from Poppy and not do anything to put her off today, because of it being my fault last time." Rose suddenly turned round to face me. "I even did my hair in that bun at school to show you that I was going to act like a proper ballet student... Only then the boys made me so mad that I had to pull it out..."

Jasmine suddenly interrupted. "So *can* Poppy show you the dance, Miss Coralie? Please?"

Miss Coralie looked as though she didn't know what on earth was happening.

"You should *see* her!" Rose suddenly blurted out. "She's mega!"

Miss Coralie frowned. "What dance?"

"The one you've started teaching the exam girls," said Rose. "Go on, Poppy, show her."

I couldn't work out how Rose knew that I'd learned the dance. Was she a mind-reader or something?

"You've learned the exam dance?" asked Miss Coralie, looking as puzzled as I felt.

"Jasmine showed me," I said quietly.

"Go *on*!" said Rose, as though she was my mum. "Do it how you did it in the cloakroom."

"You...*saw* me?"

She was grinning. "Yeah, I was hiding in the

toilet, watching through the crack where the hinges are! You looked like a proper ballerina. Go *on!*"

Miss Coralie flapped her hand and looked a bit irritated with Rose. Her eyes were on me. "Are you telling me that you've learned the exam dance right through and that you know it thoroughly?"

I nodded.

She looked at her watch for ages, as if she couldn't tell the time properly, then suddenly said, "All right... Just very quickly then..." She gave Mrs. Marsden a really sharp nod and turned back to me. "I'll count you in, Poppy."

Mrs. Marsden played the introduction. The music gave me a shock because I'd never heard it before and I hadn't imagined it would be so beautiful. It made the room feel like a stage, full of lights that swayed and glittered.

"*One* and *two* and *three* and *four*..."

It was a brilliant feeling because there was no

need to concentrate on the counts any more now. In fact, there was no need to concentrate on anything. The music did all the work, I just danced and danced...

As I held the last position, Rose started clapping and whooping. I hardly dared to look at Miss Coralie but, when I did, I saw that her eyes were bright and dark at the same time.

"Lovely, Poppy," she said slowly. "Lovely. I truly didn't know you had it in you!"

"So, can she do the exam then?" asked Rose, dropping to her knees right in front of Miss Coralie and doing praying hands.

Mrs. Marsden let out a giggle and I noticed the corners of Miss Coralie's mouth turning up. But then she suddenly looked worried and spoke quickly. "Did you post the letter of application yet, Mrs. Marsden?"

Out of the corner of my eye, I saw Jasmine's shoulders go up and heard her do a little gasp. She must have been thinking exactly the same thing as me. Now that Miss Coralie thought I was good enough, it would be absolutely terrible if it was too late.

Mrs. Marsden reached down into her handbag and yanked out a brown envelope. At the same time, a piece of paper fluttered out and landed at my feet. I didn't look at it because I was watching Mrs. Marsden. She straightened up, waved the envelope in front of our noses, grinned and said, "You're in luck. I forgot to post the envelope at lunchtime!"

"What a relief!" said Miss Coralie, taking the envelope from Mrs. Marsden and slitting it open with her finger. "I'll put your name down, Poppy."

"Oh, thank you!" I cried. At least, that's what I tried to say, but my mouth was all dry again, so it just came out like a little squeak.

And then I happened to look down and see what was written on the piece of paper that had flown out of Mrs. Marsden's handbag. It was the list of names that Miss Coralie had read out last week – the girls who she'd chosen for the exam. I reached down and picked it up and, as I handed it back to Mrs. Marsden, I read them very quickly…

Lottie Carroll
Immy Pearson
Tamsyn Waters
Sophie James?
Isobel Brooks
Jasmine Ayed
Poppy Vernon?

I managed to keep my gasp inside. So I *was* on the list. My name was one of the ones with a question mark. I'd tell Jasmine later. But, for now, I could only smile and smile as all my old sadness fizzled away and a whirlwind of happiness started whizzing around inside my tummy. I *had* been good enough. Miss Coralie would have picked me if I hadn't messed up so badly in that one lesson.

Jasmine put her arm around me and said, "I knew you could do it, Poppy." Then Rose got up and surprised me by giving me a hug.

"And so did I!" she said loudly.

"What a lucky girl you are, Poppy," said Mrs. Marsden, "having two such good friends!"

It was funny, because only a few minutes ago Rose hadn't felt anything like a friend. But now she really did.

"Off you go then," said Miss Coralie, shooing us away with her hands. "I've got another class waiting, you know."

Five minutes later we were walking downstairs together.

"I've just realized something," said Rose.

"What?"

"We're all flowers, aren't we? Poppy, Rose and Jasmine!"

Jasmine and I looked at each other with laughing eyes. "Are you thinking what I'm thinking?" I asked her.

"*Waltz of the Flowers!*" we both said together.

Jasmine turned to Rose. "Do you want to be part of the dance we've made up to Poppy's most favourite piece of music in the whole world?"

"No, I'd only spoil it," said Rose. "I'm so rubbish at ballet… But you can invite me round and I'll watch you two doing it."

"Yeah, let's go and ask Mum right now!" I said.

"And you can tell her your brilliant news!" said Jasmine, dropping her bag and sticking both thumbs up, she was so happy.

Without thinking I pressed my thumb against hers.

"Hey, what about me?" said Rose, yanking my school shoes out of my other hand and making me join thumbs with her. Then she pressed her other thumb against Jasmine's so we made a triple thumb-thumb.

My eyes met Jasmine's and we burst out laughing. Then Rose broke free and raced off down the spiral staircase crying "Geronimo!" at the top of her voice.

Jasmine and I followed behind and, for once, I couldn't hear the splitching echoey sound that our footsteps were making, because we were laughing so loudly.

Basic Ballet Positions

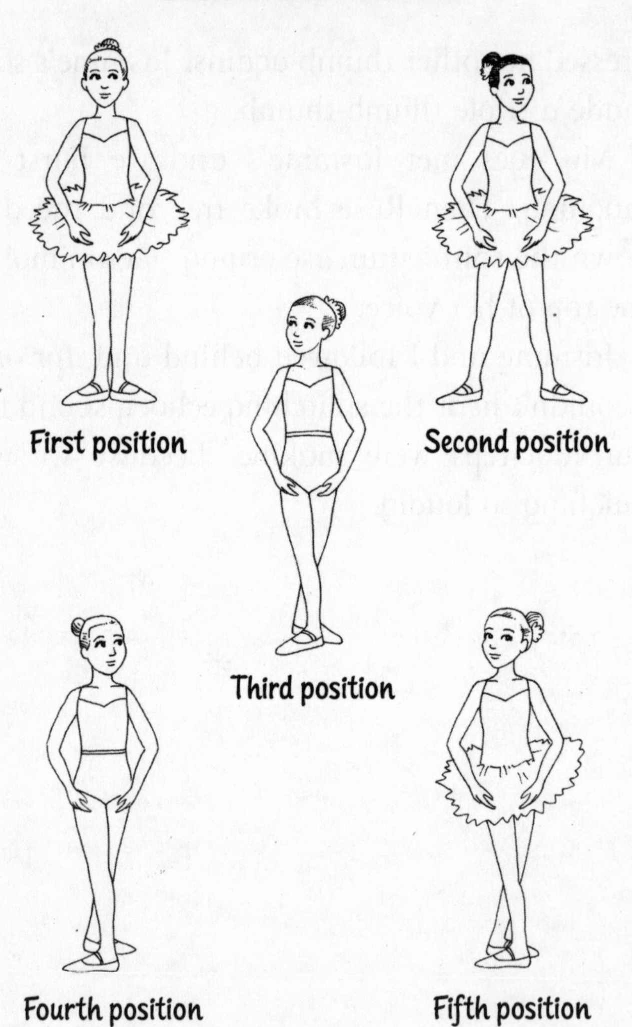

Ballet words are mostly in French, which makes them more magical. But when you're learning, it's nice to know what they mean too. Here are some of the words that all Miss Coralie's students have to learn:

adage The name for the slow steps in the centre of the room, away from the *barre.*

arabesque A beautiful balance on one leg.

assemblé A jump where the feet come together at the end.

battement dégagé A foot exercise at the *barre to* get beautiful toes.

battement tendu Another foot exercise where you stretch your foot until it points.

chassé A soft smooth slide of the feet.

echappé This one's impossible to describe, but it's like your feet escaping from each other!

fifth position croisé When you are facing, say the *left* corner, with your feet in fifth position, and your front foot is the *right* foot.

fouetté This step is so fast your feet are in a blur! You do it to prepare for *pirouettes.*

grand battement High kick!

jeté A spring where you land on the opposite foot. Rose loves these!

pas de bourrée Tiny little steps to the side, like a mouse.

pas de chat A cat hop from one foot to the other.

plié This is the first step we do in class. You have to bend your knees slowly and make sure your feet are turned right out, with your heels firmly planted on the floor for as long as possible.

port de bras Arm movements, which Poppy is good at.

révérence The curtsey at the end of class.

rond de jambe This is where you make a circle with your leg.

sissonne A scissor step.

sissonne en arrière A scissor step going backwards. This is really hard!

sissonne en avant A scissor step going forwards.

soubresaut A jump off two feet, pointing your feet hard in the air.

temps levé A step and sweep up the other leg then jump.

turnout You have to stand with your legs and feet and hips all opened out and pointing to the side, not the front. This is the most important thing in ballet that everyone learns right from the start.